Steph Sullivan

Blubeari's Very Different Summer in 2020

Illustrated by
Kris Lillyman

With special thanks to all the hard working school teachers and NHS key workers during the 2020 COVID pandemic.

BluBeari noticed a change at home, the hoomans didn't rush about so much and they didn't leave the house.... the pandemic had arrived like a tornado.

The hospitals had to prepare for more poorly people, and my daily life changed too – I had a job – I was to stand at the window and wave, to show everyone my family cared.

The hoomans clapped outside, once a week at 8.00 o'clock on a Thursday to say thank you to the hospitals and the NHS... we all had rainbows of hope.

The big hooman boss in London, in Parliament, was now making all the decisions and we all had to stay at home....

BUT FROM MY WINDOW...

I noticed Max drawing shapes with chalk on the path, but at the end of each day, with his dad's help, he washed it away with a watering can.

Mike and Jenna went jogging around the block, to help mend Jenna's poorly knee, and Clare likes to exercise too. I see her jogging past our house two or three times per week, even if it's raining. I think she is preparing to run a race for charity.

Toby and Sophie planted sunflowers which grew in the warm summer sun. The plants grew very tall with lovely bright yellow flowers the size of dinner plates.

I watched the plants grow stronger in our garden, the beautiful coloured flowers and some vegetables. In the herb garden I could see mint, chives, bay leaves and thyme and little round tomatoes that ripen in the warm sunshine...

My hooman made delicious tomato chutney to go with the cheese - very yummy

I saw Steph and Barry get their cycles from the garage and cycle off to the shops. They are often gone for ages and one day I spotted some blackberries and apples that had been picked in the woods...

...I am sure Steph made a delicious crumble for dinner that night

My hoomans worked at a desk in the study. They had video calls on the computer with family members and work friends to stay in touch. I could hear the laughter and one day they had a quiz... it made us all feel happy.

Careyanne lives around the corner, I can only just see her house if I twist my head.

She is a very clever hooman because she makes masks.

The big boss in London said that all hooman's had to wear masks covering their nose and mouth when they go outside. My favourite mask has lots of rainbow coloured spots.

I spot Jenny walking her dog. Jenny and Tim take it in turns during the week to walk Buddy, but at weekends I spot them walking him together and for much longer, Buddy loves the longer walk.

I try and hide because I'm sure he would nibble my ears and pull my tail.

After a while I noticed that Holly and Sean didn't come and stay. I normally give up my bed for them, although I didn't miss Indy the dog, as she does nibble my ears and pull my tail. I really hope we see them soon, because we all miss them.

As the summer draws to an end, I've been moved back to my bed with my friends Patch, Cornelius Fox and Daisy and I've told them all about...

The End